D1391603

This edition published by Parragon in 2009
Parragon
Queen Street House
4 Queen Street
Bath BA1 1HE, UK

ISBN 978-1-4075-8189-7

Printed in China

Beauty and the Beast

Getting to Know You

By Lisa Ann Marsoli • Illustrated by the Disney Storybook Artists

PaRRagon

Bath · New York · Singapore · Hong Kong · Cologne · Delhi · Melbourne

"Maybe the Beast has a heart after all," thought Belle. That very day, he had rescued her from a pack of wolves in the forest. Even though he was angry with Belle for leaving the castle, he had risked his own life to save hers.

"Maybe I could try a little harder to be his friend," she told herself.

Mrs Potts, Lumiere and Cogsworth were hopeful. If the Beast and Belle fell in love, the spell that enchanted them would be broken – and they would all be human again!

That night, Mrs Potts went to the Beast's room. "Master, it's such a chilly night," she began. "Why not have a nice hot drink in front of the fireplace? I'm sure Belle would love some company."

The Beast stomped into the sitting room and settled himself in a chair by the fireplace.

Belle looked up from her book. "Good evening," she said.

The Beast did his best to smile politely.

Belle went back to her reading until she was startled by a loud *slurp*. She glanced at the Beast and saw that he had a hot-chocolate mustache above his mouth. He was messy as well as noisy!

After a nudge from Mrs Potts, the Beast stopped drinking, wiped his face, and slumped unhappily in his chair.

"Why don't I read you a story?" Belle suggested. "'Once upon a time, there was an old woodcutter –'"

"That sounds so boring!" interrupted the Beast.

Mrs Potts said gently, "Is there another story you could read to us?"

Belle found a tale filled with fire-breathing dragons and brave knights. The Beast sat on the edge of his seat, listening to every word. And when he drank his cocoa, he took care to sip instead of slurp.

The next day, Lumiere and Cogsworth decided to play matchmaker, too.

"What a beautiful day for a walk!" Cogsworth said after breakfast.

"Walking is only useful when you have somewhere to go!" remarked the Beast.

But before Belle and the Beast knew it, they were bundled into winter capes and gloves and herded outdoors.

The couple walked along in uncomfortable silence. Then they came to a mud puddle.

"A gentleman would carry me over," Belle thought. Clearly, the Beast wasn't a gentleman.

"Oh, well, here goes!" she thought as she waded through the mud.

Soon the wind picked up, and it started to snow. "It looks like a bad storm is coming," the Beast warned. "We'd better get back while we can still see where we're going."

Quite unexpectedly, the Beast took Belle's hand and led her through the blizzard.

Lumiere and Cogsworth were watching out the window as the two approached, holding hands. It looked so romantic!

"It seems as if you and the Master are getting to know each other better," said Mrs Potts as she helped Belle out of her muddy clothes.

"I suppose," Belle answered. "There is so much about him that's gruff and rude . . . yet he's full of surprises."

In another part of the castle, the Beast told Cogsworth, "Belle can be rather boring and proper. But then she walked through the mud without complaining. And she didn't act scared at all when we were caught in the storm. She's . . . kind of surprising."

That afternoon, Mrs Potts prepared a lovely lunch for Belle and the Beast.

"Remember, Master," Lumiere coached, "young ladies appreciate politeness."

"Be patient with him, Belle," begged Mrs Potts. "The Master's manners aren't always what they should be – but he's trying!"

Once settled at the table, Belle smiled and the Beast forced out a grin. Both were tired from trying so hard to get along with each other.

The Beast picked up a chicken leg and began to devour it.

But after Belle placed her napkin in her lap, the Beast hurriedly grabbed his own napkin and did the same.

"Isn't this lunch delicious?" asked Belle.

"Mmpffgrl," answered the Beast, his mouth stuffed with food.

Just then, he noticed that his napkin had fallen on the floor. He ducked down to get it – and accidentally tipped the table over! A roll soared across the table toward Belle.

"Uh-oh," thought the Beast. Even *he* knew that throwing food was not polite. He was about to apologize when he saw Belle smile. To his surprise, she pitched the roll right back at him!

When Mrs Potts, Lumiere, and Cogsworth came to check on the pair, they couldn't believe their eyes. The room was a mess, and even more peculiar – Belle and the Beast were laughing!

Mrs Potts smiled and said, "I think they discovered what we forgot: the best way to make friends is to relax and be yourself!"

Later that night, Belle patiently taught the Beast how to dance. He listened carefully to everything she told him, and soon the two were gliding across the dance floor . . . in step with each other at last.